Best Stories for
Six-Year-Olds

Best Stories for Six-Year-Olds
First Published by Bloomsbury Publishing Plc in 1997
38 Soho Square, London W1V 5DF

Enid Blyton

Copyright © Text Enid Blyton Limited
Copyright © Illustrations John Eastwood 1997

ISBN 0 7475 3226 5

Printed in England by Clays Ltd, St Ives plc

10 9 8 7

Cover design Mandy Sherliker

Best Stories for
Six-Year-Olds

Enid Blyton
Pictures by John Eastwood

BLOOMSBURY
CHILDREN'S
BOOKS

Contents

Dear Children

My mother was Enid Blyton and when I was a little girl I thought that she wrote all her stories especially for me. Every night she read me a bedtime story and sometimes we read it together, a page by me then two pages by her.

I hope that you will like this story collection. Some of the stories are about witches, fairies and magic. Long ago, people did not know about science and the reasons why things happen. If something bad happened they thought it was caused by an evil spell cast by a witch or a goblin. If everything went well, they imagined that a good fairy had brought them luck. The little magic people could be good or bad and human people were very careful never to anger them.

When I was your age, I helped my mother to decorate a small tree just like the girl did in the story, The Little Christmas Tree. I have shown my children how to do it and this year I shall show my grand-children. It is hard work threading peanut necklaces but the birds will be so happy to have their own Christmas tree.

With love from
Gillian

The Fox and the Six Cats

There were once six cats who all belonged to an old lady called Miss Two-Shoes. There was a brown cat, a black cat, a white one, a ginger one, a tabby one, and one that was every colour mixed.

Every day for their dinner Miss Two-Shoes put out six dishes of boiled fish and milk. The cats loved fish, and ate their dinners hungrily, always wishing for more.

'If only we knew where these fish come from, we might be able to go and get some,' said the black cat, cleaning her whiskers carefully.

'I know where they live!' said the ginger cat. 'They live in the river that runs in the field at the bottom of our garden! Last night, when I was prowling about there, I saw a man with a long rod and line. He threw the line into the river, and very soon, when he pulled it out again, there was a wriggling fish on the end.'

'Ho!' said the white cat, yawning widely. 'So that's where the fish come from, is it? Well, I don't see how we can catch any, unless we have a rod and line ourselves!'

All the cats had listened to what the ginger cat had said, and each had made up his mind that he would go that night, all by himself, and watch the fisherman at work.

So when night fell all the cats started off for the river, and none of them saw each other, for they trod so quietly on their velvet paws.

The fisherman was there. He had baited

his line, and was just casting it into the wide river. Then he felt in his pocket for his pipe, for he loved to smoke whilst he was waiting in the moonlight for the fish to bite. But he had left his pipe in his cottage at the other end of the field.

'Bother!' he said crossly. 'I must either go without my smoke or walk back to my cottage. Well, I will balance my rod carefully here, and go quickly to fetch my pipe. I don't suppose any fish will bite yet.'

He put his rod down and set off to walk to his cottage; and, do you know, he had hardly taken ten steps before a big fish snapped at the bait! The hook stuck into his mouth and it was caught!

Then it began to wriggle and struggle, and the six watching cats suddenly saw it jumping in and out of the water. Each of them darted forward to take the fish, and how cross they were when they saw the others!

'Quick!' said the black cat, pouncing on the rod and holding it. 'One of you reel in the line.'

The ginger cat wound in the line and pulled the fish nearer. The white cat fetched the landing net to catch the fish in. The tabby helped to hold it, whilst the brown cat shouted directions all the time. The sixth cat ran to each in turn, giving a paw here and a paw there. They were all as excited as could be.

The fish pulled hard. The rod bent nearly in two. The black cat found it quite difficult to hold, and was half afraid she would be pulled into the water.

The ginger cat wound the line in steadily, and the fish was pulled nearer and nearer to the bank. Then the white cat and the tabby tried to put the landing net over it, and very soon they managed to. The fish was caught! It slipped into the net, the cats lifted it ashore, and the big fish lay shining in the moonlight.

'The fish is mine!' said the black cat. 'I held the rod!'

'No, it's mine!' said the ginger one. 'I reeled in the line!'

'Well, I fetched the landing-net!' said the white cat.

'And I helped to hold it!' said the tabby.

'I told you all what to do!' said the sixth one. 'Besides, I'm sure I saw the fish first. It should be mine.'

Then they all began to quarrel hard, and a fox, who was passing that way, heard them, and came to see what was the matter. When he saw the big fish lying there he was pleased, and made up his mind to get it for himself.

'Now, what's the matter?' he asked. 'Come, come, do not make this noise.'

'We each of us want the fish,' said the black cat. 'We don't know who should have it.'

'Well, I will be your judge,' said the fox. 'Now, I have heard that you all have beautiful voices, and often sing to the moon. I will hear you all sing, and then whichever of you has the loveliest voice shall have the fish.'

The cats agreed, for each secretly thought that his own voice was far the best.

'Very well,' said the sly fox. 'Now I will hear you all together. Sit up straight, fix your eyes on the moon, and sing your most beautiful song to her for two minutes without stopping. Don't take your eyes from the moon or that will count a mark against you.'

The cats all sat up straight, looked up at the moon and began to caterwaul. Oh, what a fearful noise it was! The fox thought it was dreadful; but did he wait to judge the singing? Not he! All the cats were looking hard at the moon and saw nothing but that, so the artful fox quietly picked up the fish and ran off with it, chuckling to himself as he heard the ugly song behind him.

For quite three minutes the cats sang

their best, and then, becoming tired, they looked down to ask the fox which of them had won. But he wasn't there! Nor was the fish!

'Oh, the scoundrel! Oh, the rascal! Oh, the scamp!' cried all the cats angrily. 'He has stolen the fish from us!'

Then, oh, dear me! The fisherman returned, and when he found the six cats howling dismally, and his rod and line all disarranged, he was angry! He sent them mewing away.

'If only we had been sensible and shared the big fish between us we should be eating it now!' said the black cat. 'How silly we are!'

And they were, weren't they?

The Surprising Saucepan

Once, when Nippy the goblin tiptoed by Dame Dozy's window, he saw her magic saucepan sitting on the kitchen stove.

Now this was a marvellous saucepan, because you had only to drop a bit of potato peel into it, and a tea leaf or two, and then say what you wanted for dinner, and the saucepan would at once cook you a stew, or a boiled apple dumpling, or anything else you asked for!

Nippy stopped when he saw that saucepan. He had nothing in his larder that night for his supper, nothing at all.

He was very hungry. Suppose he borrowed that saucepan for an hour or two? Dame Dozy would never know!

He popped his head in at the window. Nobody there. He went to the back door. There was a sheet of paper pinned to it. Nippy read what it said. 'Back at seven o'clock, signed DD. Ooooh, that's three hours ahead! Time for me to borrow the saucepan, get it to cook me a tasty stew, and a pudding afterwards, and take it back without anyone knowing. What a chance!'

He hopped in at the window and took the saucepan off the stove. It wasn't a very big one. Nippy wondered if he ought to wrap it up in paper so that no one would see him carrying a saucepan. They might wonder where he had got it.

Then a good idea came to him. 'I'll wear it as a hat!' he thought. 'It's a red saucepan, and really will look quite like a hat. Yes – it fits me well!'

So, wearing the saucepan, he hopped out of the window again and went across the common to his home.

But the saucepan began to feel a bit heavy. It had felt so light at first. Now it quite weighed down his head.

Nippy moved it a little, and it fell right over his nose! 'Bother you, Saucepan!' he said, and tried to get it off.

But it seemed to get heavier and heavier, and poor Nippy couldn't lift it off his head. He stopped still and tried his hardest.

'It *is* getting heavier – and it's getting bigger, too!' he said, in a fright. 'Oh my, oh my, it's over my shoulders now. I must get it off, I must, I must!'

But by now it was so terribly heavy that he couldn't even stand up. He had to sit down. The saucepan had grown so big that it was now down to his waist!

Poor Nippy. He bowed down lower and lower under the heavy weight, and soon the saucepan reached the ground. Nippy couldn't be seen at all! He was completely hidden under the saucepan!

He began to cry. 'What shall I do? I can't get out! It's dark under here and I'm frightened. Oh, get away, you horrid saucepan, how dare you behave like this!'

The saucepan stopped growing. It settled down over Nippy, and stayed quite still and quiet. Nippy hit it with his fists, but it took no notice at all. It just sat there and waited patiently.

'Perhaps it will grow small and light again after a while,' thought Nippy hopefully.

But it didn't. So Nippy had to stay there, underneath. There was nothing else he could do.

Now when Dame Dozy came home she missed her saucepan at once.

She told Mother Daws who was with her. 'My saucepan's gone! Never mind, there's some bread and cheese in the larder. We'll have that for our supper.'

'But, Dame Dozy, don't you want to go and find your magic saucepan?' cried Mother Daws. 'Why, it's very, very valuable. You must really find the thief.'

'No hurry,' said Dame Dozy, getting the bread and cheese. 'My saucepan can look after itself. It's got a good way with thieves. I never worry about that saucepan of mine!'

She didn't. She and Mother Daws had a good meal, then Mother Daws went home. Dame Dozy went to bed and slept well.

But poor Nippy didn't sleep at all! The ground was damp and cold. He couldn't see a single star because of the big saucepan over him. He was very hungry and thirsty. How he hated that sauccpan!

Now, in the morning, some pixies and elves came walking over the common. They were surprised to see an enormous red saucepan upside down on the common.

'Look at that!' they cried. 'What's it doing here? Let's move it.'

But they couldn't. It was far too heavy.

'Oh, do move it and let me out!' begged Nippy. 'Quick, let me out!'

The little folk were surprised to hear Nippy's voice. They stood looking at the saucepan.

'It's Dame Dozy's saucepan!' suddenly cried a pixie. 'But it's gone big! We'd better tell her!'

'No, don't, don't!' wailed Nippy, scared.

But the elves and pixies had run off to Dame Dozy's cottage. She wasn't at all surprised to see them or to hear what they had to say.

'I was expecting someone to come along and tell me where my saucepan was,' she said. 'It has a very good way of its own with little robbers! I'll come and get it.'

So she went to the common. She tapped on the saucepan.

'Who's below?' she asked in a stern voice.

'N-n-n-n-nippy!' answered Nippy, in a small voice. 'I j-j-j-just b-b-borrowed your s-s-saucepan for a bit, Dame Dozy, and it did this to me.'

'A very good thing to do,' said Dame Dozy. 'I hope it will be a lesson to you, Nippy, to keep your hands off things that don't belong to you unless you get permission first. I've a good mind to leave you here all day!'

But she didn't. She made her red saucepan go small again and set poor Nippy free.

'You be careful of saucepans in future!' she said.

And poor Nippy is so scared of them he won't even use his own at home. He boils his potatoes in his kettle.

Tibbles and the
Big Grey Goose

Tibbles was a little tabby cat. She had four tiny kittens in a round basket by the kitchen fire, and she was very, very proud of them.

The cook was very kind to Tibbles. She gave her a saucer of bread and milk in the morning, gravy and bread at dinner time, and fish and milk at tea time. So, you see, Tibbles had plenty to eat, and didn't need to catch anything for herself.

Outside in the garden lived two brown thrushes, Speckly and Freckly. They loved one another very much and they had built a fine nest in the hawthorn tree outside the kitchen window. Speckly laid four pretty eggs, and then sat on them all day long. Freckly went out to find food for her, and very often he pecked up the crumbs that the cook put outside the window.

Soon the eggs hatched out and four little baby birds lay in the nest. They grew fast and when they had their downy feathers on, they looked lovely.

And then Tibbles the cat spoilt everything! She found the nest one morning when she was climbing the tree, and she took all those four tiny birds away. She wasn't a bit hungry because cook had given her a very big dinner; she just left them on the lawn for Whiskers, the next-door cat, to eat. Wasn't it unkind of her?

Freckly and Speckly, the two thrushes, were terribly upset. They flew round Tibbles' head and tried their best to peck her. They scolded her, and flapped their wings at her, but she didn't seem a bit ashamed.

Speckly and Freckly built another nest. It was in the chestnut tree this time, and they thought they were quite safe from Tibbles there. But no – Tibbles soon spied it, and she climbed up to see if there were any little birds in it. But there were only eggs, so she climbed down again.

'Whatever shall we do?' asked Speckly, in alarm. 'As soon as our eggs hatch that horrid cat will come and steal away our little ones again. What can we do to stop her?'

'I really don't know,' said Freckly. 'I think I'll go and ask the wise old goose who lives over the fence. She may be able to help us.'

So he flew off to the grey goose, and told her all about Tibbles. The goose listened and hissed loudly when she heard about the stolen baby thrushes.

'Don't worry,' she cackled at last. 'I will give that cat such a fright that she will never touch your family again.'

Freckly flew back to his little brown wife, and told her not to worry. Then he went back to see what the grey goose was going to do. Ho, but she was a very clever bird!

She waddled through the gate in the fence and walked right up to the kitchen door. She poked her long neck inside, and saw that there was no one in the kitchen. Then she walked straight in and went to the basket where Tibbles' four kittens lay. She picked one up in her big beak and out she went with it, through the fence gate and back to her shed. She put the mewing kitten down in a corner and went back to fetch another.

When she had taken three away, and was going back for the last one, she met Tibbles.

'Oh, where are my three little kittens?' cried Tibbles, in a dreadful way. 'There's only one left!'

'Ss-ss-ss-ss-ss!' said the grey goose, and walked into the kitchen. To Tibbles' great surprise and dismay she picked the last kitten up in her beak and went off with it.

'What are you doing?' cried Tibbles, in a rage. 'Give me back

my kitten at once.'

But the grey goose took no notice. She flapped her strong wings whenever Tibbles tried to come near, and wouldn't say anything but 'Ss-ss-ss-ss-ss!' very loudly.

Tibbles followed her to the shed. The goose put the last kitten down by the others, and then hissed the cat out of the shed, and shut the door with her beak. The kittens mewed loudly. Tibbles scratched at the door and mewed too.

'Now, Tibbles, listen to me,' said the grey goose sternly. 'You took away the thrush babies, didn't you? Well, why shouldn't I take away *your* children? If it was right for you to steal poor Freckly's babies, then it is right for me to steal yours.'

'It isn't right, it isn't right!' mewed Tibbles, in despair. 'I was wrong, I know I was wrong. I'll never do such a thing again. Only give me back my kittens, grey goose! I promise never to steal little birds again!'

'Well, you left Freckly's babies on the lawn for Whiskers to eat,' said the grey goose. 'Why shouldn't I leave your kittens here for the big grey rats to nibble?'

'Oh no, oh no!' cried Tibbles, in a worse fright than ever. 'I couldn't bear it. Let me have them back, grey goose, and I promise you I'll teach my kittens never to touch birds so long as they get plenty to eat from the cook.'

'Well, you can have them back, then,' said the grey goose, opening the door. 'You have had your lesson, and I hope you won't forget it! But mind, Tibbles – if I hear from Freckly the thrush, that you have been up to any wicked tricks again, I'll come and steal your kittens, as sure as I've got two wings.'

'I'll be good, I'll be *very* good!' said Tibbles running to her kittens. She picked them up one by one in her mouth, and very soon they were all back again in their warm basket by the kitchen fire.

And I'm sure you will be very glad to know that Speckly and Freckly had a fine family of young birds and brought them all up safely. Tibbles was far too much afraid of the big grey goose to break her promise.

Look Out for the Snowman

Mother Tuppeny was puzzled. She had twelve hens and, quite suddenly, they had almost stopped laying eggs for her.

'They have been laying so well,' she said to Mr Peeko next door. 'And now they hardly lay at all. What do you think is the matter with them? Shall I give them some medicine, or scold them, or what?'

'No, no,' said Mr Peeko. 'Your hens look healthy enough, Mother Tuppeny. Perhaps your children have been running in and out, taking the eggs?'

'Oh, no. They always bring them to me

when they find any in the nests,' said Mother Tuppeny. 'It's a great loss, Mr Peeko – I use such a lot of eggs for the children, you know. I don't know what to give them for breakfast now.'

'Now you listen to me, Mother Tuppeny,' said Mr Peeko, thinking hard, 'I believe a thief may be coming in the night and stealing your eggs. You leave two eggs in one of the nests, and see if they are there the next morning.'

So Mother Tuppeny left two eggs in the nest and looked for them the next morning. They were gone! What a shame! She ran crying to Mr Peeko.

'Those two eggs have gone – and there are none at all in the boxes. It's a thief who comes, Mr Peeko. What shall I do?'

'You go to Mr Plod, the policeman, and tell him all about it,' said Mr Peeko. 'He'll know what to do.'

So Mother Tuppeny went to Mr Plod. He listened gravely, then took out his big black notebook. 'Now you listen carefully to me and do exactly as I tell you, Mother

Tuppeny,' he said. 'You go home and tell your children to make a nice big snowman near your hen house, and to leave it there tonight. And if you see me come into your garden when the moon is up, don't take any notice.'

So Mother Tuppeny told her children to go and make a fine snowman in her garden by the hen house, and they rushed out in delight.

Soon a great big snowman was built there, with a big round head, a long white body, stones for eyes and buttons, and a twig for his mouth. Mother Tuppeny gave the children one of her old hats and an old shawl to dress him in.

'It's a snow-woman now, not a snowman,' cried the children. 'Oh, look, Mother, isn't she lovely?'

'Yes, lovely,' said Mother Tuppeny, laughing at the funny sight of the old snow-woman with her hat and shawl on. 'Now come along in and have tea. It will soon be dark.'

They left the snow-woman in the garden

and went in to tea. When it got dark Mother Tuppeny thought she heard foot-steps in the garden and she guessed it was Mr Plod.

It was. He went down to the hen house and found the snow-woman. He flashed his torch on her and smiled. What a funny-looking creature!

Mr Plod knocked the old snow-woman down so that there was nothing left of her. Then he stood himself in her place, with a white coat over his uniform. He put the old hat on his head, and dragged the red shawl round him. Then he stood quite still.

When the children lifted the curtain and peered out into the moonlight before they went to bed, they laughed.

'Look! There's our old snow-woman out there all alone! How funny she looks!'

'She looks taller than when we built her,' said one of the boys.

'But how could she be?' said the other children. 'Snow-women don't grow!'

But, of course, theirs *had* grown, because Mr Plod was quite a bit taller than the

snow-woman they had built. He stood
there very patiently, waiting and waiting.

Nobody came for a long, long time. Then
from over the wall at the bottom came a
little knobbly figure. Mr Plod tried to see
who it was.

'Well, well – it's that nasty mean little
Knobbly Goblin!' said Mr Plod to himself.
'I've often thought he was up to mischief –
and so he is!'

The Knobbly Goblin crept to the hen

house. He suddenly saw the snowman – or what he thought was a snowman – and he stopped in fright. Then he laughed a little goblin laugh.

'Ho, ho! You're only a snowman! You thought you could frighten me, standing there, watching. But you can't!'

He went into the hen house and came out with a bag full of eggs. Ha, ha! What a lovely lot!

He went up to the snowman. 'Silly old snowman! Wouldn't you like to tell tales of me? But you can't!'

And then, to the Knobbly Goblin's horror, an arm shot out from the snowman and a deep voice said, 'You just come along with me!'

He was held tightly in a big hand, and then he was shaken. 'Put down those eggs. You're a thief!' said the snowman.

The Knobbly Goblin was so frightened that he dropped the eggs. Luckily they fell into the snow and didn't break.

'P-p-p-please let me g-g-g-go,' he begged. 'Snowman, who are you? I've never met a live one before.'

Mr Plod didn't answer. He took the goblin to the police station – and there Knobbly saw that it was Mr Plod, the policeman, who had got him. Ooooooh!

Mr Plod went to see Mother Tuppeny the next day. 'I've scolded the thief,' he told her. 'It was that Knobbly Goblin. I've sent him away, and I've made him pay a fine of ten golden pieces to me. Here they are!

They will help to pay for all the eggs he has stolen. I was that snowman, Mother Tuppeny!'

'Oh – how I wish I'd seen you all dressed up!' cried Mother Tuppeny. 'The children couldn't *think* what had happened to their snow-woman this morning. They were quite sad about her.'

'You buy them some sweets,' said Mr Plod. 'And tell them how I put on the hat and shawl. They won't mind a bit then!'

They didn't, of course. They laughed when they heard about it.

As for Knobbly, he simply can't bear the sight of a snowman now!

The Wonderful
Four-leaved Clover

Mollie wanted some good luck. She said she hadn't had any for a long time. Her sums were always wrong, she had lost her silver thimble, and, worst of all, her little kitten had run away and hadn't come back.

'I'm having very bad luck,' said Mollie, sadly. 'I wish I could get some good luck for a change, Mummy.'

'Well, see if you can find a four-leaved clover then,' said Mummy. 'They bring good luck, you know. Go into the garden and see if you can find one.'

Mollie thought that was a very good idea.

Out she went, and sat down on the dry grass. Little clover leaves were all around her, and Mollie began to hunt carefully. How she hunted! She looked at nearly three hundred leaves, but they all had three leaflets only. Wasn't it disappointing?

'Dinner time, dear!' called Mummy, and Mollie ran indoors. 'Well, did you find a four-leaved clover?' asked Mummy.

'No,' said Mollie. 'Isn't it disappointing, Mummy? Do you think it's any good looking much longer?'

'You might look in the dark green patch of clover at the bottom of the garden,' said Mummy. 'There may be a four-leaved one there.'

So after dinner Mollie began hunting again – and wasn't it splendid, she found a perfectly lovely four-leaved clover, as big and strong as could be! She picked it and ran indoors with it.

'Hurrah, Mummy! I've found one! What shall I do with it?'

'Press it in one of your books,' said Mummy, smiling. 'Ah, now you will have good luck, Mollie!'

Mollie was just pressing it between the pages of a book when she heard one of her friends outside calling her.

'Mollie! Mollie! Come and play!'

She shut the book, and hurried out. In the garden was Hilda, and she waved to Mollie.

'Where's Peter?' asked Mollie. 'I thought he was coming too.'

'He can't,' said Hilda. 'His mother is very ill, and he is so unhappy because she is in bed that he says he couldn't possibly come and play.'

'Poor Peter!' said Mollie. 'I'm glad *my* mummy isn't ill! Once she was, and the doctor came and I had to be as quiet as a mouse. I do hope Peter's mummy will be better soon.'

'Peter says he wishes he could go and buy a nice piece of good luck,' said Hilda. 'Then he would give it to his mother and she would get better! But you can't buy good luck. It just comes.'

'Ooh!' said Mollie, suddenly. 'I've got

some good luck! I found it just now.'

'What do you mean?' asked Hilda. 'You can't find good luck, can you?'

'It's a four-leaved clover,' said Mollie. 'Wait and I'll show it to you.'

She ran indoors and brought out the clover leaf to show Hilda. Then a great idea came into her mind.

'I'll go and give it to Peter,' she said. 'He wants good luck more than I do. His mother is sure to get better if he has a piece of good luck!'

'What a fine idea!' said Hilda. 'Come on, let's go!'

The two little girls ran down the lane with the clover leaf. They went across the fields, and soon came to Peter's house. They saw Peter in the garden and called to him.

'Sh!' said Peter. 'Don't make a noise. My mummy is trying to go to sleep.'

Poor Peter! His
eyes were red with
crying. He couldn't
bear his mother to
be ill, and he was
very sad.

'Peter!' said Mollie.
'Look! I've brought you
some good luck!' She gave him the four-
leaved clover.

'Ooh!' said Peter, in surprise. 'It's a lucky
clover leaf! Wherever did you get it?'

'I found it in the garden,' said Mollie.
'You can have it.'

'But don't you want good luck yourself?'
asked Peter.

'Yes, I do, but you want it more than I do!'
said kind-hearted Mollie. Peter thanked
her very much.

'I shall slip it into my mummy's hand and
then she is sure to get better!' he said.
Mollie and Hilda said goodbye and ran off.

On the way home Mollie passed Elm-Tree
Farm, and at the door stood the farmer's

wife, Mrs Apple.

'Mollie! Mollie!' she called. 'Come here a moment!'

Mollie ran to her, and Mrs Apple took her into the kitchen. By the fire was a and in the basket was Chippy the cat and four of the loveliest black kittens you could wish to see.

'Oh, aren't they darlings!' cried Mollie. 'They are just like the little one I lost.'

'Well dear, if your mother will let you have one, you can choose a kitten from the basket,' said Mrs Apple. 'I know you are a kind little girl and love kittens, so I should like you to have one. Run home and ask Mother. If she says yes, you can come tomorrow and choose one.'

How happy Mollie was! She raced home and told her mother what Mrs Apple had said.

'But I thought you were in the garden!' said Mummy, surprised. 'How was it you were near the farm? Why did you go there?'

'Well, Mummy, I took my good-luck clover to Peter,' said Mollie. 'His mother is ill and he does so badly want some good luck so that she can get well. And as I came back Mrs Apple saw me and called me. Wasn't it lucky, Mummy? And oh, isn't it queer? – I went to give away my good luck, and yet I got some after I had given it away!'

Mummy kissed her.

'A kind heart brings much more good luck than a four-leaved clover!' she said. 'You're a generous little girl, dear, and I'm proud of you. You deserve your kitten! You shall go to the farm tomorrow, and choose one for yourself!'

Wasn't that lovely? Mollie chose one with a white tip to its tail and proudly took it home – and waiting in the garden for her was Peter, looking very happy.

'Mollie, I've come to tell you that my mummy is better, and the doctor says she can get up tomorrow. I'm sure it was because you gave me your lucky clover!'

'I'm *so* glad!' said Mollie. 'Look, Peter, I've got some good luck too, even though I gave it away to you – Mrs Apple has given me this dear little kitten!'

'You deserve it, Mollie,' said Peter, 'because you're the kindest girl I ever knew!'

And *I* think she deserved it too, don't you?

The Very Proud Doll

Esmeralda was a very fine doll. She had curly golden hair, big blue eyes that opened and shut, legs that could walk, and a beautiful dress of red silk.

She was given to Ann on her birthday, and Ann thought she was very grand. Ann hadn't very many nice toys, so Esmeralda was her best one, and she made a great fuss of her.

'I wish I had a pram to wheel you about in, a chair for you to sit in, and a nice bed for you to sleep in,' said Ann. 'But I haven't. I'll make you a soft bed out of a cardboard box with a piece of Mummy's old blanket inside, Esmeralda. It won't be very grand, but it will be warm and comfortable.'

Esmeralda watched Ann get the box and put a piece of blanket in. She thought it was the horridest bed she had ever seen, not nearly good enough for a grand doll like herself. Ann put her into the box bed and covered her up with a piece of blanket.

'There,' she said. 'Sleep well.'

When the nursery was in darkness, Esmeralda sat up. The toys looked out of the cupboard and by the flickering firelight they could see how cross she looked. She jumped out of her bed and stamped her foot.

'Oh!' she said. 'Fancy not having a proper bed for me! I won't stay here! I'll run away! I'm much too grand a doll to put up with a bed like this, and with toys like *you*!'

She glared at the toys who were walking out of the cupboard and they stopped in surprise.

'What's the matter with us?' asked the toys, quite hurt.

'Matter enough!' said the doll. 'Why, you're dirty and old. Look at yourself, Teddy Bear! Your fur is worn away and one of your eyes is crooked. And look at that bunny – he's lost his tail and he's been in the coal shed, by the look of him.'

'Well, well,' said the bunny, sitting down and looking at Esmeralda, 'here's a grand lady for you! Don't you know, Esmeralda, that you are lucky to come to a nursery where the little girl loves her toys and plays with them? You might have been given to a child who broke you at once, or who put you in a corner and forgot all about you.'

'Pooh!' said Esmeralda, rudely. 'Nobody could forget *me*! I'm one of the finest dolls in the world! It's a disgraceful thing that I haven't even a proper bed to sleep in. Why, at the shop that sold me I was put into a bed with pink curtains and pink blankets each night!'

'Don't be silly,' said the bear, turning his back on her. 'If you're not content with this nice warm nursery, and with dear little Ann to love you, you'd better go away. *We* don't want you, I can tell you!'

'Very well, then, I *will* run away,' said Esmeralda in a temper. 'I shall soon find someone who will treat me as I ought to be treated.'

With that she flounced out of the door and down the stairs. Out into the garden she went, and then stopped to think what she should do. She didn't quite know where to go. She thought of the big dog she had seen from the window. She would go to his kennel and offer to live with him. So down the gardens she went and soon came to Spot's wooden kennel. She walked inside and made Spot jump with surprise.

'I'm Esmeralda, Ann's grand new doll,' she said. 'She hasn't got a proper bed for me, only a silly cardboard box, so I've come to live with you.'

'There isn't room in my kennel for stupid dolls,' said Spot, growling. 'Ann's a kind little girl, and I'm sure the box she gave you is the best she could manage. Go home or I'll bite you, you vain creature!'

He snapped at Esmeralda and tore a bit

out of her red silk frock. She ran out of the kennel in a great hurry, almost crying with rage.

'Rude creature!' she thought. 'I'll go to the hens. They will let me cuddle into their warm feathers.'

She went to where a hen slept in a coop, with twelve yellow chicks under her warm wings. Esmeralda woke her up by tapping her on the beak.

'Wake up,' she said. 'I've come to sleep with you. I'm Ann's grand new doll, but she's only given me a horrid cardboard box to sleep in, so I've run away.'

'Well, run away again!' said the hen, crossly. 'Ann's a nice little girl, and I'm sure she's done her best for you. You've woken up my chicks, and you're a silly vain creature to think I want you here!'

The hen pecked at Esmeralda and tore a big piece of lace from her frock. The doll gave a cry and ran away as fast as she could.

'Nasty bird!' she sobbed. 'I should have thought she would have been glad to have a grand doll like me for company.'

In the garden shed, fast asleep, lay Puss in a round basket. Esmeralda heard her breathing, and made up her mind to creep in beside her without waking her up. So she went up to the basket and tried to slip in beside the warm cat.

Puss woke up in a fright and put out her claws. 'Ooh!' screamed Esmeralda. 'Let me go! I'm only a doll!'

'What do you want here, then, frightening me?' hissed Puss. 'Ann gave you a nice bed,

and you should be sleeping there. It serves you right to have your frock torn to rags and your face scratched. Go away before I scratch you again!'

Esmeralda ran away fast, and didn't see a muddy puddle in front of her. Splash! She fell right into it, and very wet and cold it was!

'I'm going back to the nursery and to my nice cardboard bed and the kind toys,' she sobbed. 'I was silly to run away.'

She went back to the nursery, and how surprised the toys were to see her so wet and ragged. They saw that she was unhappy, and when she had said she was sorry for being so silly, they were all very kind to her.

The teddy bear helped to dry her in front of the fire, and the bunny tucked her up in her cardboard bed.

'Sleep well,' they said. 'We will take care of you, and in the morning Ann will mend your frock and love you.'

Sure enough, Ann did just as the toys had said. She was so surprised and sorry to find Esmeralda's beautiful frock torn and she wondered what had happened.

'Never mind,' she said, hugging Esmeralda lovingly. 'I'll mend your frock for you, and you shall sit in my chair with me whilst I do it, Esmeralda.'

So the doll was happy again – but whenever she forgets herself, and begins to be vain and grand, the toys shake their heads and say: 'You're too fine for us, Esmeralda. You'd better go out to the dog, or the hens, or to the cat.'

Then Esmeralda turns very red, and begs their pardon. One day she will be a really nice doll – and I shouldn't wonder if Ann buys her a proper doll's bed for Christmas. Won't she be pleased?

The Mean Old Man

Once upon a time there was a mean old man who wouldn't pay his bills. He owed Dame Rustle a lot of money for his newspapers. He owed Mr Pork pounds and pounds for his meat. Mother Cluck sent him in a bill for milk and eggs time after time, but it was never paid. Really, it was dreadful!

One day they all put their heads together and laid a little plan. They bought a come-back spell from Witch Heyho and took bits of it back to their shops.

And the next day, when Dame Rustle gave a newspaper to old Mister Mean, she tucked a bit of the come-back spell into it. When Mr Pork sold him a string of sausages, he tucked a come-back spell into them too, and when Mother Cluck let Mister Mean have a basket of new-laid eggs she carefully put a come-back spell at the bottom.

Well, old Mister Mean set off home, carrying the basket of eggs, the sausages in paper, and the morning newspaper. But before he had got very far a curious thing happened. The come-back spell began to work!

It worked on the newspaper first. The paper grew small legs and tried to get away from under Mister Mean's arm! Mister Mean could not think why

it kept slipping. He kept pushing it back under his arm – but still that newspaper wriggled and wriggled and at last it fell to the ground. No sooner did it feel its feet there than

it tore off down the
pavement as fast
as it could go,
running back to
Dame Rustle's!

'Gracious!' said
Mister Mean in
surprise. 'How the
wind is taking that
paper along, to be sure.'

Well, the next thing that happened was
most annoying to Mister Mean. The come-
back spell began to work in the sausages,
and they wriggled out of their paper
wrapping, which fell to the ground. Mister
Mean stopped to pick it up – and, hey
presto! that string of sausages leapt to the
ground and tore off on tiny legs as fast as
could be. All the dogs in the street barked
to see them rushing along like a large
brown caterpillar – but they knew better
than to touch sausages with a come-back
spell in them.

'Jumping pigs!' said Mister Mean in the
greatest alarm. 'Now, what's the meaning of

that? Look at those sausages! Do they think they are in for a race or what? Something funny is about this morning – or else I'm dreaming!'

He pinched himself hard to see if he was dreaming – but the pinch hurt so much that he knew he was wide awake. So on he went again, wondering what could be the matter with everything.

'Anyhow, the eggs are all right,' he said, looking down at them. But even as he spoke the come-back spell began to work in them, too. One by one those eggs grew chicken legs and climbed up to the rim of the basket, ready to jump out!

'Oh no, you don't!' said Mister Mean, grabbing at the top egg. 'No jumping about like that, eggs, or you will get broken.'

But the eggs took no notice of Mister Mean. One by one they jumped out of the basket and tore back to Mother Cluck's as fast as they could. It was a most astonishing sight to see.

Mister Mean was furious. 'There's some spell at work,' he cried. 'Someone's playing a trick on me!'

'Perhaps, Mister Mean,' said Mrs Twinkle-toes, who was just nearby, 'perhaps you haven't paid for those things. They have gone back to be sold to someone who *will* pay for them.'

Mister Mean went home in a rage. He wasn't going to pay his bills till he wanted to. Nobody could make him take his money out of the bank if he didn't mean to!

But, oh dear! What a life he led the next few days! His new hat jumped clean off his head and hurried back to the hatter's. His new shoes wriggled off his feet and ran back to the shoe shop with such a clatter that everyone turned to see what was making the noise – and of course they saw old Mister Mean standing in his stockinged feet looking as wild as could be – and, dear me, he had such a big hole in one toe.

Even the bananas he bought hopped out of the bag they were in and galloped back to the greengrocer's. Soon the people of the town followed Mister Mean when he did his shopping, so that they could see the strange sight of everything racing back to the shops afterwards.

Well, Mister Mean knew there was nothing else to be done but to pay his bills. So he took some money out of the bank and paid them all, every one. Then his goods stopped behaving in such a strange manner and stayed in their bags and baskets till he got home.

And you may be sure they will behave all right just so long as he pays his bills – but as the shopkeepers still have some of the come-back spell left, they will play old Mister Mean some more tricks if he begins to be mean again.

Witch Heyho still has plenty of come-back spells to sell, so if you know of anyone who needs one, just send a message to her!

The Dandelion Clock

O nce upon a time there was a fine dandelion plant that lived in a field. It put up many flowers – but one after another they were eaten by the brown horses that slept in the field each night.

At last the dandelion plant put up a golden flower bigger and finer than any before. The horses did not eat it, for they had found some very juicy grass at the other end of the field, and they did not visit the hedge where the dandelion lived. So the flower grew tall.

The bees came to it. So did many little

flies. The flower lasted for five whole days, and then it closed its pretty petals and hid its head in its green leaves. It stayed hidden there for a few days, and then once more it straightened out its long stalk, which had grown even taller. And lo and behold, the dandelion's golden head had turned white! All the gold had gone.

'You do look different,' said a little copper beetle, hurrying by.

'My head is full of seed now, precious seed!' said the dandelion. 'I have thirty-one seeds to send away on the wind – and that means, little beetle, thirty-one new dandelion plants!'

'Wonderful!' said the beetle, and ran down a hole.

The dandelion head fluffed itself out into a beautiful clock. You should have seen it! It was round and white and soft, like a full, silvery moon. It stood there shining softly in the hedge, waiting for the wind to come and puff all the seeds away.

But before the wind came someone else came – and that was a little girl. She saw the dandelion clock there and she squealed in delight.

'What a beautiful clock! I must blow it to tell the time!' So she picked the clock and began to puff.

'One o'clock! Two o'clock! Three o'clock! Oh! The fluff is all gone. It's three o'clock!'

The little girl threw away the stalk and went dancing away. And what happened to all the seeds?

A pretty goldfinch came by and saw them blowing away, all the thirty-one. He twittered to his companions, and the flock came flying down. 'Dandelion seeds!' sang the goldfinch. 'Take them, brothers! We have feasted on thistledown today, and now here are some dandelion seeds.'

They ate all they could see – twenty of them! Then off they flew. Now there were only eleven of the seeds left. 'Never mind!' sighed the plant, and it rustled its leaves together. 'That will be eleven new plants some day.'

The eleven seeds flew off. Each tiny seed had a little parachute to help it to fly. They

swung through the air, enjoying the sunshine and the wind. Two flew down to
earth to look for a resting place, but a little
mouse was there and he caught them. He
ate the seeds and then carried the fluff to
his nest to make it cosy. So now there were
only nine left.

The nine seeds flew on and on, over the
fields and hedges. Three floated downwards
– and a tiny pixie caught them and sewed
them on to her pointed cap. They made a
lovely trimming and she was very pleased
with it.

Now there were only six seeds, and they
floated high on the wind. Two flew into a

squirrel's hole and caught on the bark of the tree. The squirrel saw them and licked them off. Down his throat they went, and that left only four – four little dandelion seeds, adventuring through the air, blown up and down and round about by all the autumn breezes!

One fell to earth and was eaten by a brown sparrow. Another fell down a chimney and was burnt in the fire. Now there were only two left.

They floated onwards. One came to a pond and fell there. A fish saw it floating on the water, its little parachute looking like wings – and the fish thought the seed was a fly, and snapped at it. That was the end of that little seed. Only one was left. It flew for a long while, soaring up high, and then sinking down low.

And at last it rested on the ground, a tiny, tired seed, its parachute falling to bits. It lay there, not moving, for there was now no wind at all. It was just outside a worm-hole. That night the worm came out of its hole and wriggled about on the grass.

When it went back again it glided over the dandelion seed, and the tiny seed stuck to the worm's slimy body. It went into the hole with the worm.

And there it grew! Yes – it really did! It put out a little root. It put out a tiny green shoot – and when the spring came, there was a small dandelion plant growing out of the wormhole!

'Now, how did that dandelion get there?' wondered the little girl in whose garden the wormhole was. 'I like dandelions. I shall let it grow and give me some golden flowers.'

So the dandelion grew, and was happy and content in the warm spring sunshine and soft rain. And before long it had seven fine white clocks, all ready to be puffed.

The little girl puffed them – and off went the seed. I wonder if any will fall in your garden? Perhaps they will – and you will see a tiny plant growing up, and find golden flowers, as round as pennies, shining in the sun!

The Poor Stray Dog

There was a once stray dog that nobody owned. He had no name, and no home. He lived in the woods, and found what he could to eat. At night he used to run out and visit the dustbins that stood in the backyards of houses. Sometimes he could push off the lids and find a bone inside.

Often he caught a rat for his dinner, and once he found three pieces of bread thrown away by a tramp. That was a feast indeed for the poor stray dog! But more often than not he went hungry, and he was very thin, so that his ribs showed through his brown coat.

People were not kind to the stray dog. They shouted at him if he came near them. They hit him whenever they could. Then he would put his tail down and run for his life, growling. He thought that people were his enemies, and he longed to bite one of them.

One day he went through the wood, sniffing for food as usual. When he came near to the big pond, from which he drank, he stopped, growling. Someone was there! It was a little boy, sailing a boat. The dog did not like boys. They threw stones at him and they yelled unkind things.

The dog went a little nearer. The boy did not see him. The dog wondered if he could get a good bite at the boy. That would pay back many a blow he had had from the children!

He crept nearer and nearer to the little boy and made up his mind to bite his plump little leg. But suddenly something happened! The boy reached for his boat – and fell right into the water! The pool was very deep, and the boy could not swim. He shouted and struggled, and the dog watched in surprise.

Why didn't the boy swim? The dog had often swum across the pool, and thought all creatures could do the same. At first he was pleased to see the boy struggling in the water – then a strange feeling came into his heart. He felt as if he *must* jump in and take the little boy out!

So, into the pool he jumped, caught hold of the boy's coat with his big teeth and swam with the child to the bank. He pulled him onto the grass, and then shook himself. A thousand silver drops flew out of his wet coat. He waited for the boy to shake himself too, but the child lay still, panting for breath. Then he sat up and reached out his hand to the dog.

'You kind, good dog!' he said, and tried to stroke him. But the dog backed away, growling. He thought the boy meant to get hold of him and hit him. No one had ever spoken kindly to him before, and he ran away through the wood.

When he met his friends, the wild,

poaching cat, and the old striped badger, he told them what had happened. They stared at him in surprise.

'How foolish to be kind to one of our enemies!' said the cat, putting out her sharp claws. 'What sense is there in that? The boy will only throw stones at you the next time he sees you.'

'I know,' said the dog, quite puzzled at himself. 'But I couldn't help jumping in to save him, somehow. I *was* going to bite

him, you know – and then I found myself swimming to the bank with him!'

'You are certainly a foolish creature,' said the badger, lumbering off on his big paws. 'It doesn't pay to be kind, if you are a wild animal, or a stray one. You should be fierce and cruel.'

The dog thought they were right and he was sorry he had saved the little boy. He ran off alone, and hunted for food. As he came back, late that night, a terrible thing happened to him – he ran straight into a steel trap set there to catch animals in the wood.

Click! The cruel steel teeth closed round his paw, and the dog howled in pain and fright. He dragged at the trap, but he could *not* get his paw away. It was held tightly. The poor stray dog lifted up his brown head and howled dismally. Who had set that trap he wondered. Maybe that boy he had saved! How he wished he had not saved him from the pool in the wood! The badger was right. It did not pay to be kind.

The dog howled again and again in pain

and fright. Far away, in a small cottage, a little boy sat up in bed and listened.

'Oh dear, that's a dog in pain!' he thought. 'I wonder if it's caught in one of those cruel traps that have been set in the wood? Just suppose it was that kind stray dog that saved me from the pool, and then ran away! I can't bear it! I must go and see!'

The little boy slipped out of bed, dressed himself quickly, and crept from the cottage. He made his way to the wood and, guided by the dog's howls, came to where the stray dog was held fast by the paw.

The moon shone down and showed him the dog. The boy gave a cry of pity, and went to him at once, the animal bared its teeth and growled, but the boy took no notice. Quickly he pressed back the spring of the trap and the dog took out his paw. He was about to limp off when the boy called him.

'Come here! You must come home with me and let me bathe your paw, or it will go bad and you may lose it.'

The dog paused. The boy went up to him and picked him up in his arms. He was such a skinny creature that he was quite easy to carry. He carried the dog all the way home, and set him down by the kitchen fire.

The dog didn't know what to think. His paw hurt him, and he wanted to bite some one – but he couldn't bite this boy! So he let himself be put down on a soft rug, and he lay there whilst the boy lighted a candle and got a bowl of warm water. Then, very gently, the dog's paw was bathed, and a cool ointment put on it. Then the boy wrapped up its paw in old handkerchief and gave the dog some milk to drink, and a big biscuit to eat.

'Now I'm going to bed,' said the boy to the dog. 'You can stay here, old chap. You saved me from that deep pool this morning – and I've saved you from a trap tonight! You were kind to me, and I've been able to be kind to you! Isn't that fine? It always pays to be kind, you know. That's what my mother says.'

The dog lay by the warm fire and thought hard. The boy said it paid to be kind – but the badger said it didn't. Who was right? The boy must be – because he had gone to save a dog in pain. The little stray dog blinked his brown eyes in the firelight and thought lovingly of the boy. No one had ever been kind to him before. It was a lovely feeling.

The next day the boy's mother was astonished to find the stray dog in front of her fire. But when the boy told her what had happened in the night, she was very sorry for the dog. She stroked him gently and said: 'Poor dog! Poor dog!'

The dog wagged his tail and looked up at her. Two kind people! What luck for him!

'He is half-starved,' said the boy's mother. 'Poor creature. He has no collar, so he must be a stray.'

'Mother, he saved me from drowning yesterday,' said the boy. 'He is a brave, kind dog even though he is only a stray. Do you think I might keep him for my own?'

'Yes, if you like,' said his mother. So the

boy fetched a collar for the dog, and then gave him a fine breakfast. After that he bound up the hurt paw again, and gave the dog a good brushing.

'You'll be a fine fellow when you are fatter and cleaner,' said the boy. 'You have the loveliest eyes that I ever saw!'

The dog was very happy. He limped about after the boy, and would not let him out of his sight. He licked his hand whenever he could and wagged his tail hard. He could hardly believe that the boy wanted him to live with him and be his dog.

That afternoon he limped to the woods with the boy, who had to fetch some firewood for his mother. The dog saw his two friends, the poaching cat and the badger, and went up to them, wagging his tail.

'You have a collar on!' said the badger in disgust. 'You belong to our enemies! For shame!'

'You are becoming tame!' said the wild cat, spitting at him. 'You are no longer wild like us. Shame on you!'

'I came to tell you,' said the dog, earnestly.

'You were wrong when you said it was foolish to be kind. Kindness is a great thing, the greatest thing I know, though I am only a dog. If I had not been kind I should not be as happy as I am now.'

'Foolish creature!' said the badger in disgust, and he shuffled off.

'Traitor!' hissed the cat, and sprang lightly away. The dog was sad – but, when he heard the boy whistling to him, he wagged his tail, and limped quickly off to join him. Better to live with a kind master, than to dwell in the woods with fierce friends!

He still lives with the boy. His name is Brownie, and one of his paws is bent – the one that was caught in the trap. So, if ever you meet a dog called Brownie, with a crooked paw, you'll know his story, and can give him a pat for luck!

Santa Claus Makes a Mistake

Ellen and Jack were very excited. It was Christmas Eve, and they meant to hang up their stockings at the end of their beds. Daddy had given each of them one of his big ones, and they were very pleased.

They hung them up and then jumped into bed. 'You must go to sleep quickly,' Mother said, 'because, you know, Santa Claus won't come until you are fast asleep.'

So Ellen and Jack shut their eyes and tried to go to sleep – and it wasn't very long before they were both fast asleep and dreaming. They slept and slept, whilst the clock struck eight – and nine – and ten – and eleven! All the grown-ups went to bed. The lights were turned out. The house was dark.

The dog slept on his rug. The cat slept in her basket. Everything was quiet – except the fire in the dining room, which made a little noise now and again when the hot coals fell together.

Towards midnight Ellen woke up suddenly. She sat up in bed, wondering what had awakened her. The bedroom was dark. Jack was fast asleep. She could hear him breathing.

She listened. She thought perhaps she might have been dreaming. She switched on the light and looked round the bedroom. She looked at the end of the bed where she and Jack had hung their stockings. To her great disappointment they were quite empty.

'I wonder if that is because Santa Claus hasn't been yet,' wondered Ellen. 'Oh, how dreadful it will be if we find our stockings empty in the morning!'

Just as she was turning out the light she

heard the noise again. It was a funny noise
– a sort of scraping, kicking noise – and
then she heard a deep groan.

'Goodness gracious, whatever can it be!'
thought Ellen. She leaned over to Jack's
bed and woke him up. The scraping noise
went on and on. Jack sat up and asked
Ellen what all the noise was about.

'Jack,' said Ellen, 'I can't help thinking
it's someone stuck in the chimney down-
stairs! That's what it sounds like to me.
Oh, Jack – do you suppose it's Santa
Claus?'

'I say!' said Jack. 'I say! Suppose it is!
Suppose he's stuck! Come on quickly,
Ellen, we must go and see.'

The two children put on their dressing-
gowns and slippers, pushed open their door
and slipped down the stairs. They went
into the dining room and saw the little red
fire there. They heard the dog growling in
the kitchen, for he too had heard the
strange noises.

'Look! Look!' said Ellen, pointing to the
fireplace. 'There's a boot hanging down

the chimney! Look!'

Sure enough, there was a boot there – a big black boot – and it was on a leg – and the leg was kicking about! As the children watched, another boot came down the chimney.

'It *is* Santa Claus!' said Jack. 'He always wears big black boots in his pictures. Oh, Ellen, he's come down the wrong chimney. He'll burn himself on the fire!'

'I'll put it out before he does,' said Ellen at once. She turned on the light and went to the kitchen. She filled a jug at the tap and carried it back to the dining room. She poured water on the fire.

Sizzle-sizzle-sizzle! The fire streamed up in a cloud of thick black smoke! A startled voice from the chimney said. 'Hallo! Is anybody there? My word, this smoke is going to make me sneeze!'

'It's only Ellen and Jack,' said Jack. 'We

know you are Santa Claus. We've put the fire out so that you won't get burnt. That is why it is smoking so much. We've just poured some water on it. You've come down the wrong chimney, Santa Claus.'

'Dear, dear!' said Santa Claus. 'Have I really? You know, I have a map showing the chimneys of every house, and the right ones, leading to the children's bedrooms, are marked with a yellow cross – and tonight the wind blew my map away so I had to guess! And I've guessed wrong! I'm stuck here.'

'We could give you a pull,' said Ellen. 'Jack can take one leg and I can pull the other.'

'Go on then,' said Santa Claus. So they each took hold of a black-booted leg and pulled hard. Santa Claus came down with a rush and sat in the fireplace! A big burly man in red, with a twinkling smile and the kindest eyes the children had ever seen.

'These coals are still hot!' said Santa Claus getting up in a hurry. 'It's kind of you children to help me like this. Do you mind if I stay here for a little while till the reindeer I sent to look for my blown-away map comes back and gives it to me? I shall most likely make a few more mistakes if I go on guessing which are the right chimneys.'

'Oh, Santa Claus, of course stay as long as you like,' said Ellen. 'We'd simply love you to. I'll get some of my chocolates for you.'

'You don't suppose the grown-ups will wake up and hear me, do you?' whispered Santa Claus. 'I never know what to say to grown-ups, you know. They make me shy. It's children I like.'

'Oh, I don't think Mummy and Daddy will wake,' said Ellen. 'They sleep very soundly. The only thing that might happen is that Spot, our dog, may bark.'

'Well, go and bring him here,' said Santa Claus. 'I have a rubber bone for him, I think. It was down on my list – one dog, one rubber bone – and he might as well have it now. Dogs don't seem to hang stockings up, so I usually give them a present straight away or put it into their baskets if they are not awake.'

Jack went to fetch Spot, who seemed most delighted to see Santa Claus. He jumped up on his knee and licked his face all over.

'His tongue is as good as a sponge!' said Santa Claus. 'Here, Spot, lick this bone for a change. I really don't think my face wants washing any more.'

Jack and Ellen were so happy. It was the greatest adventure in the world to be sitting with Santa Claus, hearing him talk and laugh, and seeing him eat their chocolates.

Suddenly there came a little soft knocking at the window. Santa Claus jumped up. 'That's my reindeer come back!' he said.

He opened the window softly – and, to the children's enormous surprise, a big furry head was pushed in! It was the head of one of the reindeer. Its antlers were so big that they could not get inside the window, so the reindeer could only put in its big, soft nose, so long and velvety. In its mouth it held a large piece of paper.

'Thanks, reindeer,' said Santa Claus, and he rubbed its nose. 'I'm glad to get my map back again. Have you got a bit of sugar for the old fellow, children?'

'Of course!' said Ellen, and she ran to the sideboard where the basin of sugar was kept. She took out a handful of sugar lumps and she and Jack fed the delighted reindeer. Then Santa Claus shut the window and looked at the map. It was a most curious map, showing nothing but chimneys, and the page was marked with scores of yellow crosses.

'Well, my dears,' said Santa Claus, with a sigh, rolling up his map, 'I must be off! I have so much enjoyed this little time with you — what nice, kind creatures children are! I always did like them much better than grown-ups. I'm a bit late now, because of losing this map, so I must be off. Thanks so much for your help, and the chocolates, and the sugar lumps. Do you mind letting me out of the front door? I don't like to try that chimney again, you know.'

The children took Santa Claus to the front door and let him out. He gave them each a hug and disappeared into the night. They heard him whistling to his reindeer, and listened to the jingling of the sleigh-bells as the reindeer moved up to Santa Claus.

Ellen and Jack shut the door and went up to bed. They were so excited that they could not go to sleep.

'I'm afraid we shan't have any presents in our stockings, Ellen,' said Jack. 'Santa Claus won't come here now.'

'Well, I don't mind,' said Ellen. 'I've *seen* him – and spoken to him – and fed his reindeer – and given him a hug! I don't care if he never fills my stockings again! He's real, and I've seen him!'

It was a long time before the children did at last fall asleep. And you know, in the morning when they sat up in bed – their stockings were fuller than they had ever been before! And there were presents on the bed and on the floor, too!

'He *did* come back again!' said Ellen, in delight. 'Oh, the darling! Look what's in our stockings, Jack – the loveliest toys we've ever had!'

'Now don't say a word to anyone about us seeing Santa Claus last night, and pulling him down the chimney,' said Jack. 'He'd like us to keep it a secret, I know. Fancy him coming back again to our house – and getting the chimney right this time!'

Daddy and Mummy were *so* surprised to see what a lot of things the children had in their stockings and on the bed. 'It was a good thing you were asleep when he came,' said Mummy. 'He doesn't like children to see him, you know.'

She couldn't *think* why Ellen and Jack looked at one another and smiled, when she said that – but I know why, don't you?

The Cackling Goose

J ust outside Lord Cherry-Tree's mansion stood a tiny white cottage where Mother Dilly lived with her little girl Lilith. They lived all alone except for Cinders the black cat and Sukey the big white goose.

Lilith loved Cinders and Sukey. The cat walked by her heels all day long, and the goose always ran to meet Lilith when she went to feed it. It was a big goose and a noisy one, so noisy that very often one of Lord Cherry-Tree's footmen would come down to the little white cottage and say that his lordship's visitors complained of the noise in the early morning.

'It's a nuisance, your goose,' said the footman, who looked very grand in a red coat and breeches, with gold buttons and trimmings. 'Why don't you sell it?'

'Oh no, oh no!' said Lilith, before Mother Dilly could speak. 'She is my own dear goose, and I love her. If we sell her she will be killed and eaten.'

'Cackle, cackle, cackle!' cried the goose, who was near by.

'There it goes again,' said the footman in disgust. 'What you want to keep such a noisy bird for, I don't know. One of these days Lord Cherry-Tree will send me down to kill your goose, and that'll be the end of it.'

'I wouldn't let you!' sobbed Lilith, thinking that the footman was very unkind. 'I tell you it's *my* goose!'

'Pooh!' said the footman and went back to the big house.

Lilith ran to the goose.

'Sukey dear, please don't cackle so much!' she begged. 'I don't want you to be sent away. I've had you since you were the funniest little gosling, and I'm very fond of you. Besides, you lay us such fine big eggs, and we really couldn't do without you!'

'Cackle, cackle, cackle, cackle!' said the goose, in her very loudest voice. Lilith ran indoors and fetched a panful of food. Then the goose was quiet.

That night when her mother was asleep, Lilith crept outside and called to the goose.

'Sukey! Come indoors in the warm with me!' she whispered. 'Then you will be happy and won't cackle in the morning.'

So Sukey waddled indoors, happy to be with her little mistress. Lilith meant to wake up early and take Sukey out before Mother Dilly woke up – but alas, she overslept, and in the morning Mother Dilly woke up to find Sukey the goose perched on the end of her bed, saying: 'Cackle, cackle, cackle!' as fast as she could!

'Bless us!' she cried, in a fright. 'How did that goose get here? Well, I never did! It will have to go if it starts to come in the house like this, frightening the life out of me!'

'Oh Mother, don't say that!' begged Lilith. 'I brought her in last night so that she shouldn't cackle out of doors this morning and wake up Lord Cherry-Tree's visitors. Some people came yesterday in the coach. I saw them. They looked very grand too, and their dresses were shining with gems.'

'Well, well, I'm not going to have the goose indoors, however many visitors come to the big house,' said Mother Dilly shooing the goose outside.

So the next night the goose had to sleep outside, but it didn't seem to mind.

Lilith and Mother Dilly went to bed early, for they had been scrubbing and baking that day and they were tired. And my goodness me, whatever do you think? Why, in the very middle of the night, yes, when all the world was quite dark and people were fast asleep, that goose began to cackle.

Cackle! She made such a noise that it seemed as if a hundred geese were cackling! 'Cackle, cackle, cackle,' she went, 'Cackle, cackle, cackle! Cackle, cackle,

cackle, hissssssss!'

Lilith woke up with a jump. Mother Dilly sat up and groaned to think of what Lord Cherry-Tree would say.

'He'll have that bird's head cut off tomorrow as sure as I'm sitting here,' she said.

Lilith rushed outside in her little white nightgown – but she had no sooner put her feet outside the door than she stopped in surprise. She could hear voices! And then she saw the light of a lantern and heard a man say: 'We can get over the wall just here! Drat that bird with its cackling. it may wake people up!'

'Robbers!' thought Lilith, keeping as still as a stone. 'Come to steal the jewels of those grand visitors at the big house, I expect. Oh, what can I do?'

She darted back into the cottage and just stopped Mother Dilly lighting a candle.

'Don't!' she whispered. 'It's robbers. If they see a light here they'll run off and won't be caught. Mother, I'm going to go up to the house by the short way I know –

you know, by climbing up that old tree and sliding down the other side of the wall like I used to do. I'll soon be at the house and I'll wake them up. Then perhaps the robbers will be caught!'

Off she went before her mother could say a word. She climbed up the old tree she knew so well and slipped safely down the other side. Then she crept quickly between the trees and made her way softly to the big house. It was all in darkness; but Lilith knew where the footmen slept, and she took a handful of gravel and threw it against the window of their big room.

The window was thrown up and someone looked out. 'Sh!' said Lilith. 'It's me, Lilith from the cottage. There are robbers climbing over the wall. I'll go back and take their ladder away as soon as they are over and then you and the others can catch them easily in the grounds, for there is no other way of getting out, save by the gate and that's locked!'

She disappeared. The servants at once put on coats, took sticks and lanterns, and unloosed the dogs. By the time they were ready Lilith had gone back to the place where the robbers had put their ladder by the wall. There was no one there. The robbers were creeping quietly through the trees towards the big house. Lilith moved the ladder and sent it crashing to the ground. At the same time there came the barking of dogs, the cries of excited men, and the sound of running feet.

It was not long before all the robbers

were caught and locked up in the cellar. Lilith went back to bed and soon fell asleep – but not before she had hugged Sukey the goose and told her that she was a very good and clever bird, the best in all the world!

Next day Lilith was told to go to the big house to see Lord Cherry-Tree himself. She went – but with her she took Sukey the goose, tied by her leg with a string.

'I want to thank you for your bravery and goodness last night,' began Lord Cherry-Tree – but to his surprise Lilith pushed forward her goose, who at once said: 'Cackle, cackle, cackle!' very loudly indeed.

'It was my goose that caught the robbers, really,' said Lilith, proudly. 'She cackles very loudly when anything disturbs her. She is better than a watchdog, your highness.'

Lord Cherry-Tree laughed. 'So you have brought your goose for its reward, have you!' he said. 'Very well, child, it shall have a gold collar for cackling – but what reward would *you* like Lilith?'

'The only reward I would like is to be allowed to keep my goose as long as it lives,' said Lilith at once. 'I know it cackles loudly sometimes and disturbs you, your highness, but it's a good goose and I'm fond of Sukey.'

'Well, what about you and your mother going to live in the little yellow house on the hill over there?' said Lord Cherry-Tree. 'Then we shouldn't hear your goose when it cackles in the morning.'

'Oh, sir, oh, sir!' cried Lilith in delight, for the yellow house was very lovely, and had a beautiful garden. 'But how should we afford to live in such a fine house?'

'You shall have a bag of gold each year,' said Lord Cherry-Tree. 'You and your goose have saved jewels worth many thousands of pounds, and it is right that you should be well rewarded for your bravery. Go and tell your mother what I have said.'

Off ran Lilith, and the goose waddled behind her, cackling crossly because it had to go so fast. But for once the little girl took no notice – she wanted so badly to get to her mother and tell her the wonderful news.

And there they are to this very day, living happily in the little yellow house, and in the garden lives Sukey the goose, with a fine gold collar round her neck.

'Cackle, cackle, cackle!' she says, but nobody minds at all!

The Great Big Bone
(A Story by Bobs the Dog)

Once upon a time, dear children, as I was out walking, I smelt a glorious smell. I stopped and sniffed. It was a smell of bone, and it came from the hedge.

'Tails and whiskers!' I wuffed to myself. 'It must be a great big bone to have such a great big smell.' So I ran to find it – and just exactly at the same moment as I came from *my* side of the hedge, another dog, much smaller than I am, ran to get that bone from the *other* side of the hedge.

'It's *my* bone!' I growled.

'No, it's *mine!*' growled the other dog. He

took one end and I took the other, and we snarled like the beginning of a thunder-storm. It was a wonderful bone, with meat on it, and it certainly had a wonderful smell.

'Do you know, dog, I believe this bone's bad,' suddenly said the other dog to me, and he dropped his end and began to sniff along it. 'It's been here a long time, and I shouldn't be surprised if it's poisonous now. Once I ate a poisoned fish head and I was dreadfully ill. I couldn't wag my tail for three weeks.'

I dropped my end too and sniffed. That bone had a glorious smell, but it certainly was very strong indeed. I wondered if it *could* be bad. I can tell you, I didn't want to lose the wag out of *my* tail, it's too useful.

'Shall I taste the bone and *see* if it's all right?' said the little dog.

'If you like,' I said. So the dog ran his tongue over it and bit a piece of meat off. And then, whiskers and tails, dear children, he suddenly rolled over and over, gave dreadful yelps of pain and wuffed:

'Oh, fetch help, fetch
help! I'm poisoned!'
I was frightened,
I can tell you. 'Lie
there, dog,' I said.
'I'll go and fetch
my Mistress. She
will know how to
make you better.'

'Oh, quick, oh, quick!'
groaned the little dog, rolling over and
over again. 'Oh, who would have thought
that bone was so poisonous!'

I rushed off as fast as my four paws could
go. I hunted everywhere for Mistress, and
at last I found her.

'Come quickly!' I begged her. 'There's a
poor little dog in great pain through eating
a poisoned bone.'

So Mistress put on her coat and hurried
off with me to the hedge. 'He's just about
here,' I said. I scurried to the hedge – but
wags and whistles, would you believe it,
there was no little dog there – and no bone
either! They were both gone, and all that

was left was a wonderful smell of faraway bone!

'He was too little to fight you for that bone!' chuckled a robin in the hedge. 'But quite big enough to trick you! Trilla, trilla, what a duffer you are!'

And, dear children, I had no wag in my tail all that day, I was so upset. Just wait till I meet that little dog again!

Mollie Visits the Moon

Mollie had a very strange adventure one night. She was lying in bed, trying to go to sleep, but the moon shone right on to her face and she couldn't.

'You funny old moon!' she said. 'You're like a slice of melon tonight, hanging up there in the sky. I wish I could pay you a visit.'

Then suddenly a very queer thing happened. A shining pathway appeared, stretching right down from the moon to Mollie's bed, and a voice said:

'You'll be very welcome. Please come and

see me, but do you mind bringing a pail and a sponge with you. I've bumped my face against a star, and it's *so* dirty!'

Mollie jumped out of bed, and dressed herself quickly. She felt very much excited to think she was going to the moon. She couldn't see who spoke to her, but she thought it *must* be the moon himself, for there didn't seem anyone else that it could be.

'I mustn't forget to take a pail of water and my sponge,' she said, when she was dressed. So she found a pail, filled it with warm water from the tap, and put a bit of soap in the soap rack on the side of the pail.

'Now for my sponge and towel!' she said. She got those too, and then she was all ready. What an adventure, to be going to wash the moon's face!

She stepped on the shining path. It held her quite firmly, though it didn't look at all strong. Up she went, and up. It was quite easy, and not a bit slippery. Such a bright light was in her eyes that she didn't like to look up, for it dazzled her. So she went walking on, looking down at the path, till a jolly voice sounded near to her.

'Well, Mollie, here you are! Pleased to see you! I'm glad you've brought your sponge and soap. Can you see the smuts that that stupid star left on my face, when it bumped into me?'

Mollie looked up. Why, there was the moon, just near her! It had the jolliest face at one end, with two twinkling eyes looking down at her.

'Sit on my curve,' said the moon: 'You can reach my face easily then.'

So down Mollie sat, hanging her pail on the moon's lower point. She put her sponge in the water, and then sponged the moon's face. That didn't get the smuts quite off, so she put some soap on, and washed as hard as Nurse did, when Mollie's hands were dirty.

'Ooh! Ah! Ooh!' suddenly cried the moon. 'You've put the soap in my eye! Ooh! How it smarts! You bad girl! You did it on purpose!'

'Oh, I'm so sorry,' said Mollie, frightened. 'I didn't mean to. Let me wipe your eyes with my towel.'

That made it worse. The moon groaned and growled, and then began to wriggle and shake. Mollie clutched at her end, and only just saved herself from falling off. Her pail slid off, and went tumbling down through the sky.

Then the moon gave such a great heave that poor Mollie fell off too. Down she

went, and down and down and down.

'What a bump there will be soon!' she thought. 'Oh, I do hope I don't hurt myself!'

She looked down and saw the world coming nearer and nearer and nearer.

Then BUMP! She came to earth!

'Oh, I've hurt myself!' she cried. 'Oh, you horrid moon! Mummy, Mummy!'

Mollie felt someone picking her up, and she opened her eyes. There was her mother, kissing her.

'Why, darling, what were you dreaming of?' she asked. 'You've tumbled out of bed!'

'No, Mummy, I tumbled off the moon,' said Mollie. 'I put some soap in his eye, but I didn't mean to.'

'You've been dreaming!' said Mummy. 'Look, there's the moon up in the sky. It's been shining on your face, and making you dream. We'll draw the curtain, and shut him out.'

Click! The curtain shut out the cross old moon. Mollie snuggled down again, wondering if she really *had* been to the moon or not. What do *you* think?

The Little Christmas Tree

There was once a little fir tree that hated Christmas time. When it saw the snow coming it shivered and shook from top to toe.

'What's the matter?' asked a rabbit who had come out to nibble at the bark of a big tree near by.

'It's Christmas,' said the fir tree. 'It may mean nothing to you, rabbit, but it frightens me. You see, I'm big enough now to be a real proper Christmas tree at a party. I shall be pulled up by my roots, and hung up in a shop. I shall be bought and carried home. I shall have sharp spikes stuck into my stuck into my tender branches when I am decorated, and, worse than that, candles will be lit all over me. I shall be burnt, I know I shall!'

'Well, you're a funny sort of tree,' said the rabbit, in surprise. 'Most fir trees are very proud to amuse the children.'

Just then a man came by with a spade. When he saw the little fir tree he dug it up and put it into a cart. Then he carried it away to the nearest town. It trembled all the way, for it knew that its time had come. Soon it was hung outside a shop, and presently a little girl came to buy it.

'Now I shall have sharp spikes set into my branches,' groaned the tree, 'and candles will burn me.'

The little girl carried the tree home and planted it in a round bed in the garden. The fir tree was so surprised, for it had thought it would be put into a tub. 'I shan't be a Christmas tree after all!' it thought.

But it was. The little girl decorated it next day, and hung all kinds of presents on

it – but what funny
presents they were!
The tree couldn't
understand them
at all. There
were twelve bits
of coconut, eight
biscuits, ten crusts
of bread, two strings
of monkey nuts twisted
round and round its branches, six pieces of
suet and five sprays of millet seed hung all
around it!

'Well, whatever is all this for?' wondered
the tree in astonishment. He soon knew on
Christmas morning, for there came such a
rustle and flutter of wings, such a twitter
and chirping! Down flew all the birds in
the garden and perched in the branches of
the little fir tree! Robins and sparrows,
thrushes and blackbirds, starlings and tits,
finches and hedge sparrows, they all came
and pecked eagerly at the presents on his
branches.

'You're a birds' Christmas tree!' cried a

big thrush to the little tree. 'You're put out here for us! And every Christmas you'll be decorated like this, and in between times you'll grow bigger and bigger in the garden! Aren't you happy?'

'I should think I am!' cried the fir tree, and you should have heard his branches rustle from top to toe!

The Dirty Old Teddy

Once there was an old, old teddy bear in the toy cupboard. He was so old and dirty that nobody knew what colour he had once been, and he didn't even remember himself.

He only had one arm, and one of his legs was loose. His eyes were odd, because one was a black button and the other was brown. He had a hole in his back and sawdust sometimes came out of it. So you can guess he was rather a poor old thing.

But he was wise and kind and loved to make a joke, so the other toys loved him and didn't mind him being so dirty and old.

'All the same, I'm afraid he'll be thrown away into the dustbin one day,' said the blue rabbit, shaking his head. 'I'm afraid he will. He really is *so* old and dirty.'

The little girl in whose playroom the bear lived never played with the old teddy. She had a fine new one, coloured blue, with a pink ribbon round his neck, two beautiful eyes, and a growl in his middle. She loved him very much. She always pushed the old teddy away if he was near her.

One day her mother picked up the old teddy and looked at him. A little sawdust dribbled out of the hold in his back.

'Good gracious!' said Joan's mother. 'This old teddy really must be thrown away. He isn't even nice enough to be given to the jumble sale.'

'Well, throw him away, then,' said Joan. 'I don't want him. He looks horrid with only one arm and a leg that wobbles, Mummy. I never play with him now.'

All the toys listened in horror. What! Throw away the poor old teddy! Oh, dear, what a terrible pity!

'Well, I'll put him in the wastepaper basket in a minute,' said her mother. She put the teddy on the table beside her and went on with her knitting. Soon the bell rang for dinner, and Joan's mother forgot about the teddy.

As soon as she had gone out of the room the toys called to the bear, 'Hurry, Teddy! Get down from the table and hide at the back of the toy cupboard!'

The bear fell off the table and limped over to the toy cupboard. He really was very frightened. He hoped that Joan's mother wouldn't remember she had left him on the table.

She didn't remember – because when she came back she had another child with her, besides Joan. A little boy clung to her hand, and she was talking to him.

'You will love staying with us, Peter dear. You shall play with Joan's toys, and have a ride on the rocking horse.'

Peter was Joan's cousin and he had come to stay with Joan for three weeks. He was a dear little boy, but very shy. The toys watched him all the afternoon. He was frightened of the rocking horse because it was so big. He liked the dolls' house because everything in it was little. He loved the top that spun round and played a tune, and he liked the train that ran on its lines.

When bedtime came, and he sat eating bread and milk in the playroom, he began to cry.

'I've left my old monkey behind,' he wept. 'I always go to bed with him. I shall be lonely without him.'

'Well, you shall have one of Joan's toys to take to bed with you,' said her mother, and she took him to the toy cupboard. 'Choose which you would like, Peter.'

Peter picked up the brown dog – and then the rabbit – and then the sailor doll – and then the blue cat. And then, quite suddenly, he saw the dirty old teddy bear looking up at him out of his odd brown and black eyes. He gave a squeal and picked him up.

'Oh, can I have this darling soft teddy?

He looks at me so kindly – and I do like his funny eyes. Oh, please, please, may I take *him* to bed with me?'

'Good gracious! It's the bear I meant to throw away in the dustbin!' said Joan's mother. 'You don't want a dirty old toy like that, surely!'

'Yes I do – yes I do!' cried Peter, and he hugged the bear hard. 'I shall cry if you don't let me have him.'

'Of course you shall have him, but if you

love him so much I shall have to mend him up a bit tomorrow,' said Joan's mother. So Peter took the old teddy to bed with him – and you simply can't imagine how happy the bear was!

He cuddled up to Peter and loved him. It was such a long, long time since he had been taken to bed by anyone. He was so happy that even his little growl came back when Peter pressed his tummy.

And next day – good gracious! Joan's mother took him and made him a new arm. She sewed on his wobbly leg. She mended the hole in his back – and she made him a beautiful blue shirt with little sleeves!

You can't think how different he looked! The other toys looked at him in amazement and joy.

'You won't go into the dustbin now, Teddy,' they said. 'You look simply lovely!' And he does, doesn't he?

The Cuckoo in the Clock

In the playroom on the wall hung a cuckoo clock. Every hour the little wooden cuckoo sprang out of the little door at the top and called 'Cuckoo!' very loudly indeed. Then it went back into its tiny room inside the clock and stayed there all by itself until the next hour came.

The wooden cuckoo was very lonely. There was nothing to do inside the clock except look at all the wheels going round, and he was tired of that. He was a most intelligent little cuckoo, and when the children talked near the clock, he listened to every word, and learnt quite a lot.

He knew when the bluebells were out in the wood, for he had heard Lulu say that she was going bluebelling. And he knew that seven times six are forty-two, because once Barbara had to say it twelve times running because she hadn't learnt it properly the day before.

So you see he was quite a wise little cuckoo, considering that he lived in a tiny room inside a clock all day long. He knew many things, and he longed to talk to someone in the big world outside.

But nobody ever came to see him. The children had heard him cuckoo so often that they didn't think anything about him, and except when the clock was dusted each morning nobody came near him at all.

And then one night a wonderful thing happened. The little fairy Pitapat asked all the toys in the toy cupboard to a party at midnight! What excitement there was!

The teddy bear, the sailor doll and the baby doll all got themselves as clean and smart as could be. The wooden Dutch doll scrubbed her rosy face clean, and the Japanese doll tied her sash in a pretty bow. The soldiers marched out of their box, and just as midnight came, the fairy Pitapat flew in at the window!

The cuckoo had to pop out at that moment to cuckoo twelve times, so he had a fine view of everything. He thought that Pitapat looked the dearest little fairy in the world – and then, dear me, his heart nearly stood still!

For Pitapat looked up at the clock, and saw him! She laughed and said: 'Oh, what a lovely little cuckoo! And what a beautiful voice he has! I must ask him to come to my party.'

She flew up to the clock, and asked the cuckoo to come to the party. He trembled with delight, and said yes, he would love to come. So down he flew among the toys and soon he was quite at home with them.

The party was in full swing and everyone was having a lovely time, when suddenly the door was slowly pushed open. Pitapat saw it first and she gave a little scream of fright.

'Quick!' she said. 'Someone's coming! Back to your cupboard, all you toys!'

The toys scuttled back to the cupboard as fast as could be, just as Whiskers, the big black cat, put his head round the door. He saw something moving and made a pounce! And oh my, he caught poor little Pitapat, who was just going to fly away out of the window.

The cuckoo had flown safely up to his little room in the clock, and he peeped out when he heard Pitapat cry out. When he saw that Whiskers had got her, he didn't know *what* to do! He was terrified of cats – but he simply couldn't bear to think that Pitapat was in danger, with no one to help her at all.

So with a very loud 'Cuckoo' indeed he flew bravely down to the floor. With his wooden beak he caught hold of Whiskers' tail and pulled and pulled and pulled. Whiskers couldn't think what it was that was tugging so hard at his tail, and he looked round to see.

In a trice the cuckoo flew to Pitapat, and picked her up in his claws. He flew to his clock, and, very much out of breath, put the little fairy down just inside his tiny room. Whiskers gave a mew of disgust when he found that the fairy had gone, and jumped out of the window.

The moon sent a ray of light to the cuckoo, and he could see Pitapat quite plainly. She looked very ill, and was as white as a snowdrop. The cuckoo felt certain that she ought to be in bed. But there was no bed in his little room!

Then he suddenly thought of the tiny bed in the small dolls' house in the toy cupboard. He flew down and asked the sailor doll to get it out for him. It was not long before he had the little bed in his beak, and was flying with it back to the clock.

He popped Pitapat into bed, and then fetched her a cup of milk from the dolls' house larder. She said she felt much better, and thanked him. Then she put her golden head down on the pillow and fell fast asleep. How pleased the cuckoo was that he had rescued her! He thought that she really was the loveliest little creature that he had ever seen.

For a whole week she stayed with him, and they talked and laughed together merrily. The cuckoo felt very sad when the week drew near to an end, for he really didn't know *what* he

would do without his
tiny friend. He knew
that he would be
lonelier than ever.

Then a wonder-
ful idea came to
him. If only Pitapat
would marry him,
they could live to-
gether always and he
wouldn't be lonely any more! But would a
fairy like to live in a tiny room inside a
clock with a funny old wooden cuckoo?
The cuckoo shook his head, and felt certain that she wouldn't. And a big tear came
into one of his eyes and rolled down his
beak.

Pitapat saw it, and ran to him. She put
her arms round his neck and begged him to
tell her why he was sad.

'I am sad and unhappy because soon you
will go away, and I shall be all alone again,'
said the cuckoo. 'I love you very much,
Pitapat, and I wish I wasn't an ugly old
wooden cuckoo with a stupid cuckooing

voice, living in a tiny room inside a clock. Perhaps if I were a beautiful robin or a singing thrush you would marry me and we would live happily ever after.'

'You aren't ugly and old!' cried the fairy, 'and your voice is the loveliest I have ever heard! You are nicer than any robin or thrush, for you are the kindest bird I have ever met! And I will marry you tomorrow, and live with you in your clock!'

Well, the cuckoo could hardly believe in his good fortune! They asked all the toys to a wedding party, and Pitapat bought the cuckoo a blue bow to wear round his neck so that he looked very grand indeed. And after the party they went back to the clock and danced a happy jig together round the little room.

'I can make this room lovely!' said the fairy happily. 'I will have blue curtains at the windows, and a tiny pot of geraniums underneath. I will get some little red chairs and a tiny table to match. Oh, we will have a lovely little house here, Cuckoo!'

She set to work, and she made the dearest

little place you ever saw. The cuckoo loved it, and one day when Pitapat had brought a new blue carpet and put it down, he was so pleased that he quite forgot to spring out of his door at ten o'clock and cuckoo!

There was no one in the playroom but Barbara, and she was most surprised to find that the cuckoo didn't come out and cuckoo. She got a chair and put it under the clock. Then she stood on it and opened the little door.

And, to her very great surprise and delight, she saw Pitapat's little room, so bright and pretty, and the cuckoo and Pitapat sitting down to a cup of cocoa and a biscuit each! Weren't they surprised to see their door open and Barbara's two big eyes looking in!

'Don't tell our secret, Barbara dear!' cried Pitapat. 'We are so happy. *Don't* tell our secret! Please! Please!'

'I'll keep your secret,' promised Barbara. 'But please do let me peep into your dear little house each day. It is so little and lovely.'

'You can do that and welcome,' said the cuckoo, and he got up and bowed.

So every day when there is no one in the playroom Barbara peeps into the cuckoo's home in the clock; and you will be glad to know that she has kept her word – she hasn't told a single soul the secret!